Remember
life is but a dream,
make it a good one!

Renée

The GoodNight Fairy Helps Via Change Her Dream

by: Renée Frances, B.S., B.Ed., M.A.
illustrated by: Romaine Tacey
edited by: Mary Curk

*For Pauline and Skinner, my foundation,
my unwavering cheerleaders, my parents.
They would have loved this!*

~R.T.

*For all the dreamers out there, especially those
who believed in this project enough to help Kickstart it!*

Particular gratitude for the generosity of:
* Mark and Ashley Bader and family
* Fran Rozek
* Vince and Linda D'Andrea
* Rock Basacco
** Frank, Olivia, and Abigail for your on-going
support and understanding!*

In Memorium
Rock Rozek ★ *Lena Basacco*

~R.F.D.

Produced by:

Somnus
Stuff 📖

London, Ontario, Canada N6M 0C1
Distributed to the trade by
The Ingram Book Company

 child named Via
wakes up through the night.
She goes to her mommy
to make things all right.

Her dreams make her restless;
she talks in her sleep.
She tosses and turns,
and the stress makes her weep.

Miss Via may wake up
without knowing why.
Tonight she gets up
in the midst of a cry.

Her mom tries to calm her;
she wipes away tears.
The hugs and the kisses
do help quell her fears.

As her Mommy explains,
I observe from the wings,
Watching closely as Via
takes in some new things.

"Dreams can be scary
but this much I know:
Although you are frightened,
you're still in control."

"In your dreams
you can do
anything that you need.

You can jump
super high,
you can run
with great speed.

If you want
you can climb
to the top of a wall.

Simply try,
you can fly,
there's no reason to fall."

Skeptical Via, unsure and still weepy

Goes back to her bed, she's feeling quite sleepy.

Now this is my cue! I'm prepared to assist.
My colleagues and I, we're the sleep specialists!

I'm known as the Fairy
of a Good Night's Sleep.
When someone's in need,
all-night watch I will keep.

My job is to help young ones
have restful naps.
Have I visited you in the past?
Well, perhaps.

I work hard to be certain
that children like you,
Get all of the quality sleep
you need to.

Sleep is essential;
it helps your brain grow.
What are you learning?
Well, only you know.

Friendly Theta and Beta

and Delta and Alpha

Will work all night long

and together we help ya'.

And my name is REMy.

It's so nice to meet!

You dreamers are in for

a beautiful treat!

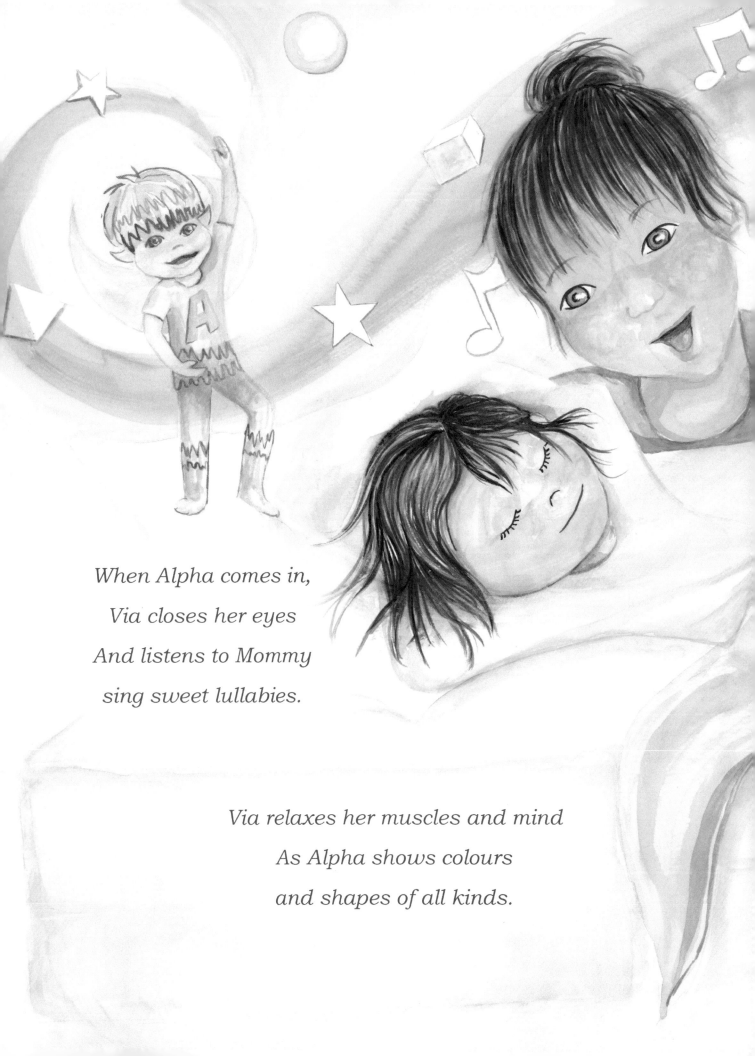

When Alpha comes in,
Via closes her eyes
And listens to Mommy
sing sweet lullabies.

Via relaxes her muscles and mind
As Alpha shows colours
and shapes of all kinds.

Next Via gets 'dozy',
her breathing slows down;
Beta's working to help
Via not move around.

When Delta comes in,
Via's sleep becomes deep.
Delta makes sure
she won't walk in her sleep.

Now Theta and I
need to get on the case
When this dream commences,
I'll be right in place.

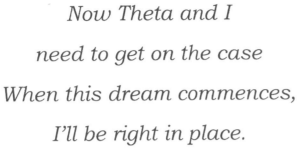

Her dream's at the beach
on a nice sunny day.
Her closest of friends
are here with her to play.

They're splashing
and running!
But wait,
what is this?

Via's not smiling. There's
something
amiss.

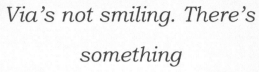

She's scared
and she's frowning,
with tears in her eyes,

Being chased by her friends
and she doesn't know why.

Now is her chance

to turn this dream around

And Via will make a big smile of that frown.

Via recalls everything she was told:

Her dream's up to her.

She's empowered and bold!

As Theta and I
coalesce with the scene,
She embraces this truth
and her friends seem less mean.

Via speaks with conviction;
her fear starts to fade.
"None of you scare me.
I'll not be afraid."

"I know that I'm dreaming.
I want to have fun
With my friends at the beach,
in the water and sun!"

She then breathes a 'sigh'
in her dream and for real.
The breath really helps.
I ask, "How do you feel?"

Not saying a word,
little Via replies,
"I'm happy! I'm sure
there's no reason to cry."

It was true; I could see that she actually felt it,

The relief that came when her worries all melted.

Although we won't eavesdrop,

she'll not be alone.

We'll let Via enjoy

this nice dream on her own.

We will be close by her
to help if she needs
A gentle reminder
to change what she sees...

From a dream that disturbs her,

making her wary,

To one that is happy

and not at all scary.

When Via awakes
in the morning she might
Remember what happened
while dreaming last night.

Then again she may not
but our work is worthwhile,
Whenever a wee one
wakes up with a smile

And starts a new day
feeling well and refreshed,
My friends and I know
that we have done our best.

So before you turn in,

do your best to retain

The knowledge that

you're the one holding the reins.

In your dreams
you're the boss!
You'll know just what to do!
But if you forget
we will help remind you.

REMy's Guide to Lucid Dreaming

PREPARE TO BECOME A LUCID DREAMER

Your dreams are real experiences over which you have a very special kind of control; none of the rules of the waking world apply in your dream world. If you are having nightmares, like Via does, it is important for you to know a few things:

★ Your dream world is yours. Think of it as your kingdom. Have fun exploring it!
★ You give everything in your dream world all of the power and meaning that it has for you. If you see a 10-foot-tall bear chasing you, you CAN 'change' it into a small stuffed animal and then ask it why it was chasing you. You may be surprised with its answer to your questions.
★ Your dream world is a **safe place** for you to learn how to deal with your frustrations or fears. Be confident in yourself and you will be able to face any challenge.

V.I.A.: *the way to* Lucid Dreaming

V = Value Your Dreams

Giving your dreams some attention throughout the day will help send the message that they are valuable. Here's what you can do to set the stage for a night of awareness:

★ Do "reality checks" throughout the day. Ask yourself, "Am I dreaming right now?" Adopting this habit will increase the likelihood that you will also check-in while you are dreaming and *voilà*, you're aware that you're in a dream.
★ Try pressing the finger of one hand through the palm of the other hand. If your finger goes through, you're dreaming. Enjoy exploring your dream world.
★ BE SURE to do a reality check before trying to walk through a wall or fly. There's no need to hurt yourself.

I = Intend to Dream

Lucid Dreaming often happens after your body has had a chance to rest and is ready to rejuvenate.

★ Be sure to turn off all screens and dim the lights at least one hour before bedtime. This will prepare your brain for sleep.
★ Go to bed as early as possible. If you need to be up for school by 7 a.m., an 8 p.m. bedtime may be perfect for you.
★ If you wake up in the night to use the washroom, go back to bed and tell yourself, "I will be aware when I am dreaming," or "I am aware when I am dreaming."

A = Aid Dream Recall

By talking or writing about your dreams, you are helping yourself remember your dreams.

★ Before going to sleep each night visualize or tell someone what you want to dream about.
★ Imagine yourself in that setting and with those people. The clearer the picture in your head the better this will work.
★ Write your dreams in a dream journal. You can use a combination of words and pictures to describe and explain your dream experiences. If you're still a bit too young to draw or write about your dreams, you can tell your family members what you dreamt about the night before. You'll be able to share stories and help each other see important patterns in your lives.

I'M DREAMING. NOW WHAT?

★ Don't get too excited or you may wake up. Tell yourself: "Stay calm," and "Focus."
★ If you feel the 'edges' of your dream world getting fuzzy, slowly turn yourself around. Spinning in place will stabilize your dream world surroundings.
★ Don't forget that you're dreaming; you'll end up slipping out of your dream before you realize it.
★ Try touching something. Walk through the grass, or sand, or mountains with bare feet. Breathe in the fresh air. Pet the mane of the unicorn that just walked up to you.
★ Test things out. Use your senses of taste, touch, sight, smell, and hearing.

WHAT DO I DO IF SOMETHING FRIGHTENS ME?

Like Via, you may experience some dreams that are scary. Don't be afraid because **you** have all the power in the situation. Here are some things that you can try:

★ Tell the scary 'thing' to go away or leave you alone. It has to listen to you.
★ Change the scary thing into something less scary - like a toy replica of itself.
★ Ask 'it' why it's there. Often, our dream characters are trying to help us. They do use symbols and figurative language that may be confusing, so be patient with them (and yourself).
★ Remember that, as always, manners matter and kindness counts. Dream characters, like people from your waking world, are like an echo: they will give back what they receive.

WHAT ELSE CAN I DO IN MY DREAM WORLD?

After doing a *reality check* and knowing that you are aware in your dream world, try a few of these things. Remember to write, draw, or tell someone about your dream experiences as soon as you wake up. As you continue to practice Lucid Dreaming your skills will grow and develop.

★ Fly
★ Walk through walls
★ Breathe underwater
★ Explore outer space
★ Transport yourself to 'anywhere' in the blink of an eye
★ Create (art, music, a new invention...)
★ Use superpowers
★ Become your favourite animal
★ Talk with the characters you meet in your dream world
★ Visit distant (or deceased) friends or relatives
★ Keep learning!

Afterword

By Dylan Tuccillo, Jared Zeizel, and Thomas Peisel
Authors of *A Field Guide to Lucid Dreaming: Mastering the Art of Oneironautics*

Dear Mom and/or Dad,

Kudos to you! By picking up this book, you've decided to empower your children and teach them that dreams are not only safe, but the very playground of the imagination. You deserve a good ole' pat on the back.

We are born dreamers. As children, we spend our days eating, pooping, and when we're done... sleeping. In fact, sleep research estimates that children will spend about 40% of their childhood asleep. The time they spend in REM sleep - the period most attributed to dreaming - is far greater than adults, averaging around 25-50% of their total sleepy time. Jealous, right? This is why, with the right environment and awesome parents (like you), we can provide them with a lifelong skill of a rich inner dream life.

Dreams are Normal

Every single person on this planet dreams (yes, that means you too) and they do so every night. It's part of who we are. It's a universal experience that links everyone on the planet. When talking to your children about dreams, introduce it as a normal part of life and something that everyone does.

We may not know what dreams are or why we have them, but science has proven this much: that we can wake up inside our dreams and change them. In other words, we can have a *lucid* dream.

What is Lucid Dreaming?

If you've never experienced it yourself, it might be difficult to wrap your head around the idea of lucid dreaming. Simply put, a lucid dream is a dream in which you are aware that you're dreaming while it's happening. It's the same attention and focus that you have at this very moment, but in a dream.

What if, when you glanced away from these words, you realized that you were in fact in a dream right now, at this very moment? You could float above the clouds, walk through walls, or go off exploring the landscape of your psyche, all with full, lucid awareness. The possibilities would be endless.

Dream Activity
Plant the Seed - What Would You Do Right Now If You Were Dreaming?
Help your child imagine the possibilities of becoming lucid by asking them, "If you were dreaming right now, what would you want to do?" Suggest some fun ideas and let them pretend. Fly? Go see a friend? Ask the moon a question?

As you know, children use their imagination all the time to play games. They're action heroes, they're throwing tea parties, or they're going on great adventures. When playing pretend, your child chooses the story, the characters and the setting. Lucid dreams work in the exact same way just with a bigger backyard and better costumes.

Not 'Just' A Dream

When your kids come running into your bedroom, complaining about the boogeyman's latest nighttime cameo, resist the urge to tell them, "It's just a dream." Dreams, especially nightmares, have a valid reality of their own and are emotionally and creatively potent. Disregarding our own dreams will only teach our children to further ignore and suppress them.

When your children are faced with a nightmare, talk openly about it during the day. Try to understand where the nightmare comes from and how they might overcome it. Perhaps you could offer suggestions for what they could do next time it happens. "If that giant monster were here right now, could we try to make friends with it? Maybe even invite it over for a tea party?" Monsters have feelings too, after all. Encouraging your kids to become lucid during a nightmare might sound like an intense activity, but if you pump the idea full of confidence and playfulness, you can present the idea as a chance for fun. Encourage your kids to follow these easy steps:

Defusing the Nightmare

1. During the day, casually rehearse the nightmare with them. This is a good time to figure out how your little ones are going to defuse a fearsome character or situation. Guide your kids to use their imaginations and role play, pretending to be the nightmare. Maybe your little ones will decide to shape-shift into an invincible dragon, or a fairy godmother. Not only is this exercise a good rehearsal, it will also put your kids into the right mindset for a lucid dream. This type of technique is usually referred to as dream incubation. Read them *The Good Night Fairy Helps Via Change Her Dream* and remind your children that they have the ability to become lucid while dreaming.

2. When a nightmare character appears in the dream, this is their opportunity to realize they're dreaming. Prepare them for this encounter by reminding them, "The next time you see the nightmare, you will know that you must be dreaming." Have them practice saying the phrase: "I'm dreaming!"

3. Stay Lucid. When your children become lucid, they should take a few deep breaths of dream air and relax. It's easy to get excited in the first few moments of a lucid dream, so much so that they might wake up. Within the dream, if they can relax and even spin slowly in a circle, this can help "anchor" the dream and stabilize the dream environment. Have your kids approach the boogeyman character and ask: "What do you want?" or "Why are you being so mean?" Follow the plan that you came up with together in step one.

4. Remember to remind them that they're safe and that it's impossible to be harmed in a dream. This confidence will help ease the fear that comes with a nightmare.

5. *Optional:* Consider giving your kids a power object. A magic wand, a bear, something that they can place under their pillow and then use in the dream world as protection. Explain to them that this object will be there to help face nightmares. "You don't have to do it alone."

Supportive Environment

A great way of helping your children's connections with their dreams is with dream sharing. You might find that by discussing your dreams, you will see both the dream and your children in a new light. A great place to share is at the breakfast table. Be sure that you partake as well by sharing your own dreams. If you had a scary dream, see if you can come up with a solution together. Asking your kids to help you brainstorm the next nightmare situation shows indirectly that they have the same power for themselves. The most important thing with dream sharing is to never judge. Be supportive and curious about their dreams.

Finally...

Children are natural lucid dreamers. They only need encouragement and the right environment to develop the skills. That's exactly what this *Good Night Fairy* book is all about. Our friend Renée has done an amazing job presenting these ideas in a fun, accessible way. She understands kids and how they think (and she's a heck of a rhymer).

Before long, you might notice something alarming: the tables have turned and your kids are teaching you how to navigate the dream world. Don't be embarrassed, it happens. After all, those little tikes are the original dreamers.

Sweet dreams!
Dylan, Jared, and Thomas

Resources:

1. http://sleepfoundation.org/sleep-topics/children-and-sleep
2. "Brain Basics: Understanding Sleep" Office of Communications and Public Liaison, National Institute of Neurological Disorders and Stroke, National Institutes of Health. Accessed December 5th 2013.

CPSIA information can be obtained at www.ICGtesting.com
Printed in the USA
LVIW01n0501230316
480296LV00007B/14